MATING WITH MALLOWS

AN EROTIC SENTIENT CANDY ROMANCE

NORA NOODLE

For my husband, who always believed I could do this.

CHAPTER 1

"Come on, Cece. Just *try* one," Miranda pleaded from her seat five feet away from mine in our shared cubicle, a glittering bonbon of a marshmallow held aloft for me. The remnants of its friend's carnage staining her tongue yellow.

It was something of a joke between my best friend and, well, herself—although she was swiftly beginning to pull all of our coworkers at our small-town paper-selling company into it as well.

As if it wasn't enough that this time of year always reminded me of when my dad walked out as a child, everyone now thought it was peak entertainment to pressure me to bend until I joined in on the consumption of their favorite pastel sweets.

I tucked an inky strand of hair behind my ear with a wrung out sigh.

I, Cecelia Anne Reynolds, did not care for sugar. Jelly beans didn't cut it for me. Neither did those little chocolate eggs stuffed with cream. But the worst were the sugar-coated marshmallows.

As they stared at me with their beady little eyes from their shrink-wrapped packaging which barely contained their edible, neon glitter-bomb bodies, I could feel their evil presence. I could taste the sickly-sweet cream within, which no hot chocolate could disguise. I could—

My thoughts were interrupted as a pink projectile careened into my cheek, landing with a muted thud on my desk.

"Miranda, I swear—" But my objections were drowned out as Todd and Anthony poked their heads into our shared cubicle, wild grins on their faces as I wiped the offending grit from the side of my face.

"It's not cute," I bit out to no one in particular.

"We only tease you because we love you," Miranda crooned. "And because no matter how many years we've been friends, I can't figure out why *candy* of all things is the one thing you can't stand. For some people, it's fish. For others, it's snakes. For you, these sweet"—she drew out the word in her charming, southern drawl—"little guys who couldn't hurt a fly."

"You know, they taste even better if you microwave them. Did you eat them straight from the package last time?" Anthony asked with a knowing grin.

Last time. A time I'd rather forget. Mom had just gotten home from work. The phone rang, but I didn't think much of it. I was too obsessed with using it as a distraction to sneak my little socked feet silently onto the shelves of the pantry so I could reach my six-year-old arms all the way to the tip-top to steal some Easter candy.

I had just blindly grabbed a packet of marshmallows, ripped it open, and was creeping back down from my perch with one in my mouth when I heard it—a wail ripping out of my mother which turned what had once been a highly coveted treat to ash in my mouth. Nothing had tasted the same since.

I ignored the jibe, retreating into myself. This wasn't the time or place for that. These weren't the people to discuss it with. If even my therapist hadn't been able to cure me … Well, I didn't need to discuss it with some coworkers glomming on to my best friend's joke.

She seemed to catch on to this, a tentative hand squeezing my knee. "Never mind that now. Let's go get some lunch." She smiled at me, pushing me towards the cafe, an apologetic curry working to soothe the small hurt as I tried—and failed—to forget the encounter.

CHAPTER 2

To say that I moved on quickly would be a gross exaggeration. The night sweats had returned, along with dreams in which I relived the worst day of my childhood over and over. What had been for years a quiet joke amongst my friends was beginning to reel back in everything I had worked so hard to forget for years.

Perhaps I should confide in Miranda about it. I knew that if she knew how deeply it affected me— that it wasn't just a dislike of the candy itself—she wouldn't pressure me like she did, but I had never been able to voice the words to her. The only ones who really knew the depths of my hurt were Mom and the child therapist I had been forced to see after the incident.

I thought about calling the mental health center —I really did—but somehow I couldn't muster the courage. They would make me talk about it, unearth all my childhood hurts. How my dad had left with Susan, moving across the country. How he never showed up for my birthday parties. Never came to a softball game. Never called. How I'd never been able to fully trust a man since.

It would be exhausting, and I was already on my last leg. I just didn't have the energy to dredge it up again, and it wasn't like previous attempts had done anything more than keep it temporarily at bay—hidden in the back of my mind but never fully forgotten.

That was how I found myself at the supermarket after work on Thursday, looking for something quick and frozen to heat up for dinner, when the candy aisle caught my eye.

There, from the shelves, they taunted me. I could never fully escape them, and a small niggling in the back of my mind urged me down there—steered my cart in their direction.

Just try one, it crooned. *Just one. And then maybe you can forget.*

I must have been losing my goddamned mind, but I followed on autopilot until I stopped in front of the shelf which was certain to be my doom.

A veritable rainbow looked back upon me. Pink. Yellow. Green. Blue. Purple. Ten different flavors and five different shapes to boot. If I were really about to do this though, I had to go with the classic combination. I had to erase the original memory from my mind, push it back as far as it would go.

I hesitantly reached for a variety pack of bunnies. Four vibrant, differently-colored little creatures stared back at me with malice in their souls. I hid the package beneath my frozen lasagna to gain some reprieve, checked out, and drove home—the weight of the marshmallows in my bag dragging me down to hell.

~~~~~~

Later that night, with a leaden stomach, I opened the grocery bag which had been unceremoniously tossed aside on my entry table in the foyer. I had to do this now, while I had the stomach and the nerve.

I stared myself down in the full-length mirror beside me, ignoring the gooseflesh dimpling my bare arms and legs in my dress. It wasn't cold in here.

I focused instead on staring deep into my emerald eyes, connecting with myself to feel grounded again. Deep breath in. Deep breath out. I could survive this. I had to.

I slipped one finger under the flap of the shrink wrap, sliding it delicately until it had loosened, taking my time to stall as best I could. The next flap came up seamlessly, and I was able to slide the cardboard tray out, revealing my inevitable, sugary demise.

I headed to the kitchen and placed the pink one on a plate. Surely, it was the most harmless color, right? I had always been a sucker for a good hot pink.

As I was about to put it in the microwave though, I gave pause. Perhaps it needed a friend. Two was a good number. Bonded in pairs. Half of the package. If things went incredibly wrong, I would still have a fallback. And if I was still truly revolted by them, I didn't *have* to eat both.

The electric blue mallow quickly followed its friend onto the plate, and without giving myself too much time to think about it, I plopped it in the microwave for twenty seconds.

The timer tick-tick-ticked its little heart out, my own matching its rhythm double-time. It got down to one second left, and my right hand reached up in anticipation of the telltale ding, when instead, an enormous explosion knocked me off my feet.

CHAPTER 3

Disoriented, I looked towards the microwave, dreading what I was going to find. Truly, tonight couldn't get any worse. The last thing I needed was to have broken my microwave and set my house on fire. It felt like a bad week was only getting worse.

But … when I looked over at the microwave, I didn't see flames. No charring. The door was just hanging open, and—

"Ah, that's better," a deep, sensual voice crooned from my left, and my head whipped around.

There, in the middle of my kitchen, stood two hulking marshmallows. No—to call them marshmallows would be an understatement. These hunks were anything but mere mallows.

Standing at least six feet tall—not including the ears—dripping with muscles, coated in a fine dusting of neon sugar, were two incredibly sexy marshmallow bunny men.

"There she is," the blue one grinned, and I recognized it as the voice I had heard earlier. My throat bobbed.

"Like what you see?" purred the pink one next to him. Deep, charcoal eyes, which I had found creepy on the inanimate mallows smoldered in my direction.

Somehow, in coming to life, they had completely transformed. Gone were the objects of my lifelong hatred. And instead, before me stood the creatures of my dreams.

"I—" I began, but Pink shushed me.

"Now, now. We've been waiting all evening for you to free us. Leaving us all alone in that cold packaging, in the pitch-black innards of your shopping bag. Tsk. Tsk."

"Naughty girl," pitched in Blue, a grin splitting his bunny face. I wanted to lick his icing whiskers off. My cheeks heated as I realized that not only was I not terrified of them, but I *wanted* them. Something primal was churning deep within me. It had been … awhile.

"I didn't m-mean—" I stammered, at a loss for words. I was still leaning on my elbows, staring up at the gooey gods above me when Pink stepped out from behind the counter.

I practically yelped as he came fully into view. Try though I might to keep my gaze firmly centered on his chest, it betrayed me, darting first to brilliantly corded thighs and up, up, up until it rested firmly on his giant cock.

Upon noticing my attentions, it rose to the same, and my insides ignited. Blue came to join, and the sight of their twin erections towering over me made my mouth into a desert ravine.

"What are we going to do with you?" Pink growled, crouching next to me, pausing to allow my hand—acting of its own accord—to reach for his bare chest. Sugary grit met my palm as I stroked down his eight-pack in amazement.

Real. This was real, and through the colored coating, I could feel the pillowy flesh beneath, giving way to my touch before springing back into place in the wake of my hand.

"Who are you?" I breathed, meeting their eyes. It was a mistake. I could see a deep longing within them which would haunt me far longer than I cared to admit.

"We've missed you, Cecelia," he whispered, before scooping me in his arms and depositing me on the countertop. "All these years, we've watched as you passed us by, never giving us a fair chance until today. Being denied the feel of your lips,"—a grainy finger traced the arc of my lower lip—"The flick of your tongue,"—it hovered over the center, in anticipation. Some part of me which couldn't resist, flung my tongue gently through my lips, tasting its divine deliciousness along the way.

"That's a good girl." I didn't need him to say it twice before I took that finger in my mouth, suckling long and hard, showing him exactly what I would do with … other things.

Blue came up on the other side of the island, firm yet gentle hands massaging my shoulders, digging into small knots I hadn't even been aware existed. A groan of pleasure escaped my lips, slipping around the candied digit still entangled there, as I relaxed into his grip.

My tongue swirled around and around, and as crystals coated it, I feared the mallows might dissolve beneath my ministrations, but they seemed to hold firm; their fluffy goodness regenerated for each bit of their deliciousness I swallowed.

"Yes," Pink crooned, removing his finger from my mouth before threading his fist into the hair on the nape of my neck. Yielding lips crashed into mine, vanilla and sugar flooding my taste buds as his tongue swirled together with my own, warm and soft and wet, just like every man I had ever been with—but so much more delectable.

He tugged on my hair to the point where I groaned, exposing my throat before peppering sugar-stubble kisses right along my pulse.

Blue's hands left my shoulders, to my protest, but I was soon silenced as they traveled, skimming my torso until they found my waist. Warm, strong fingers gripped me with purpose as Pink continued ravaging my throat.

My legs pressed together as heat flooded to that most sensitive of spots, begging for those lips, those hands—*anything*—to replace the cold countertop beneath me. It didn't stop my hips from pressing down into the stone though, searching for any sort of purchase—any relief.

"*Please*," I gasped between hitched breaths, and the mallows seemed to know exactly what to do, a choreographed Dance of the Sugar Plum Dicks, as Pink retreated, Blue rotating until he was at my front, fingers scraping the exposed skin where my dress dipped at the small of my back along the way.

He lifted me off the surface, but we didn't go far, traveling all of the ten feet it took to reach the couch in my living room. He plopped me gently onto the cushion with a command. *"Kneel."*

I did as told, and the world went dark as something silken was tied around my eyes. I thought about protesting but failed to find my voice as I felt four powdery hands lavishing my stomach, my thighs, as my clothing began to be peeled off my skin.

I almost laughed at the absurdity of it. Just hours before, I hadn't wanted to look at them, yet here I was, dying for a peek at their candied abs.

"Good girl." This time it was Blue in front of me, one finger crooked beneath my chin as he lifted it towards his lips. A harsh kiss with a little nip was all the reward I received. Until I felt Pink behind me, fingertips dancing up the insides of my thighs, parting them with one hand, even as his other hand gently coaxed the small of my back until I was on all fours between them, while they towered over me.

I licked my lips in anticipation.

"Have you ever been with two before?" Pink asked, rewarding my pliability beneath his hands with a small flick of the clit which sent a shock through my core.

"Just once," I admitted, thinking back to my college days.

A sloppy frat party, a couple of dudes I had never seen again in a bed while my then-best-friend and roommate had been having her own sexual celebration on the other side of the dorm room. One of them had been so far gone, he'd struggled to get it up, which had honestly likely been a mercy.

"Two men, a long time ago." Even I could tell how nervous I sounded.

"Well, buckle up, sweetheart," Blue chuckled. "We are no normal men."

CHAPTER 4

That was all the warning I had before they plundered me, again in perfect harmony with each other.

Even as Blue's candy cock flooded my mouth, I felt Pink nudge at my entrance, a slick, gooey coating helping to ease it in until it filled me to the hilt. It didn't stop me from gasping, crying out around the enormous, confectionary cock in my mouth—long enough to cut off my oxygen if I wasn't careful.

I had never been so full of marshmallow in my life, and something told me that this was just the beginning of this feeling.

As Pink eased out, his gelatinous tip stretching my tight pussy before slamming back into me in ecstasy, I swirled my tongue around Blue's cock, eliciting a few beads of marshmallow fluff, which I greedily swallowed before moving on him.

It was difficult, matching the rhythms of the two insatiable mallow beings penetrating either end of me, but they strove to assist me—Pink setting a pace which I could bounce along to as I used the momentum to ride his enormous sugary schlong while I sucked Blue from base to tip over and over.

I could feel his cock throbbing in my mouth as marshmallow goo tickled my tongue, a sucrose pulse inexplicably beating within the hunky beast.

To say I licked him like a lollipop seemed inappropriate in this context because he was so much more.

No mere sucker could compare to the life I felt pouring through this being. It couldn't twine its fingers into my hair. Couldn't make those little grunts of satisfaction as I oscillated along its length. Couldn't writhe beneath me as, even in my submission to these sexy beasts, I flicked and taunted and teased its cock.

No, my mallow lovers were so much more. I couldn't fathom how I'd survived my whole adulthood without this kind of attention.

Pink thrust into me dutifully, one rough hand coming around to my front to just the right …

I saw stars as his thumb pressed down on my clit, feeling the telltale trails of pink coating he was leaving behind. It flicked back up again, and I gagged lightly on Blue's erection as I struggled to remain upright, every muscle in my body tensing in contradictory ways even as I burned from within.

"Careful, sweetheart," Blue growled from above me, one hand moving from my hair to help steady my arms, even as he rode me closer, the two cocks in either end of me pinning me in place like a rotisserie chicken.

God, I contemplated how good it would feel— the twisting deep at my center even as my tongue became a cyclone around the cock in my mouth. It would be like licking an ice cream cone into oblivion but so much sweeter.

I writhed, slamming my ass up against Pink, my back arching downwards as I gave in to his dominance. Sensing my submission, Blue began to carefully ride my face. The steadying hand moved to the back of my head, bracketing it in place as I opened wide, allowing his pillowy cock access to my throat.

I felt him shudder as he plowed my mouth, the satisfaction evident as he met what was awaiting him behind my tongue. I suddenly knew I could drive him to his knees in the future with this move.

The future. I was actually considering the fact that this might be my new normal. That I might *want* more of this. No, not just want. Need. Crave. In the way an addict couldn't stay away from their drug of choice.

I undulated between their lengths, body frozen by their saccharine sex organs fucking me in ways I had never been fucked before—and couldn't survive without again.

When Pink finally tickled my clit again, I erupted, unable to hold back the river of desire which had been damming up inside me any longer. My moans of their names were muffled by Blue's cock before he slammed so hard into me that I couldn't breathe anymore, and I felt marshmallow fluff slither down my throat as he came inside me.

Pink let out a few more deep groans before I felt a warmth enter my cunt, an ooze overflowing and beginning to slide down my leg.

The marshmallow men stilled, quieting as I swallowed the remnants of Blue on the back of my tongue, letting it linger before fully accepting his fluffernut into me.

CHAPTER 5

An expectant silence filled the room, while the reality of what we had just done overcame us all. I had just fucked two living marshmallow men—the embodiments of everything I had stood to hate for a few decades—and it had changed my life.

Pink slid out of me, his marshmallow filling seeping down onto the cushion beneath me as my pussy couldn't hold it all in. Blue eased himself out of my mouth, and a gentle hand caressed my chin, lifting it to see his smiling face as he removed the blindfold with the other.

My two marshmallow princes worked together to draw me a bath, studiously avoiding the water as they lowered me in and handed me a washcloth so I could clean my aching cunt before helping me dry off and get into my pajamas.

In an unspoken agreement, all three of us slipped into bed, and I snuggled between my lovers.

Finally, I felt like I had regained a bit of myself, a bit of my voice. "That was incredible."

"Now you finally see what you've been missing, don't you?" crooned Blue, but I could hear it for what it was. Beneath the smiling tone, I felt the weight of the statement. The fact that what had once been missing would never go astray again. That something had shifted, and this … This was permanent. Or it could be, if I wanted it.

"Never again," I confirmed, stroking a reaffirming hand over his chest as I wriggled my ass in even closer to Pink, who was curled up behind me.

I saw the error of my ways. One bad experience in my past didn't have to taint my future. I could be more than the sum of other people's mistakes. I could grow and learn and start anew.

One way or another, this was going to be my future.

I would have to microwave the rest of the pack tomorrow.

Acknowledgments

Thanks to my family, without whose support I would not be here. I love you all for giving me the courage to write and the means to do so.

Thanks to you, my reader! However you stumbled upon this story, I'm glad to see you here, and I hope you enjoyed it. If you did, please leave me a review so I can bring you more in the future.

About the Author

Nora Noodle is a wife, mother, and avid romance reader. When she's not hanging out with her family, she can be found reading, writing, and plotting unending sex scenes in her head.

Made in United States
Orlando, FL
12 November 2024

53758930R00017